OLIVER, CLARENCE & VIOLET

JAMES STEVENSON

Oliver, Clarence & Violet

GREENWILLOW BOOKS
NEW YORK

Copyright © 1982 by James Stevenson

All rights reserved. No part of this book may be
reproduced or utilized in any form or by any means,
electronic or mechanical, including photocopying,
recording or by any information storage and retrieval
system, without permission in writing from the
Publisher, Greenwillow Books, a division of William Morrow
& Company, Inc., 105 Madison Avenue, New York, N.Y. 10016.

Printed in the United States of America   First Edition

1 2 3 4 5 6 7 8 9 10

Library of Congress Cataloging in Publication Data
Stevenson, James (date)
    Oliver, Clarence & Violet.
    Summary: Oliver, a beaver, decides to build a ship
and leave his pond to look for greener pastures, but
finds that all his animal friends want to accompany him.
    [1. Beavers—Fiction.   2. Animals—Fiction]   I. Title.
PZ7.S8474801   [Fic]   81-13294
ISBN 0-688-80275-3   AACR2
ISBN 0-688-84275-5 (lib. bdg.)

CONTENTS

1. Not Just Another Dam   9
2. A Safe and Sound Secret   15
3. The Secret Slips Out   21
4. Vince Lends a Hand   25
5. Strange Sounds   34
6. Ready to Set Sail   40
7. A Nice Farewell   47
8. Down the River   61
9. A Stowaway   66
10. Trouble Ahead   72
11. Turtles Don't Sniffle   81
12. Welcome Home   89

OLIVER, CLARENCE & VIOLET

1. NOT JUST ANOTHER DAM

"Watch where you're stepping!" said Clarence.

"Sorry," said Oliver. "Thought you were a rock."

"That's what you always say," said Clarence.

"That's what I always think," said Oliver.

"What's Oliver done now?" asked

Violet, coming to the edge of the pond.

"He stepped on me for the nine hundredth time," said Clarence.

"Typical," said Violet. "Furthermore, Oliver has annoyed everybody all day with his crashing and banging and splashing."

"When you're building," said

Oliver, "there's bound to be a little ruckus."

"How many dams do you have to build, anyway?" said Violet.

"Yeah," said Clarence. "You've messed up the whole pond."

"I'm not building a dam," said Oliver.

"What is it?" said Violet. "One of your yucky-looking mud-and-stick houses?"

"Nope," said Oliver.

"A bridge?" said Clarence.

"Nope," said Oliver.

"What *is* it?" said Violet.

"A secret," said Oliver.

"I know enough secrets," said Violet, "without any dumb beaver secrets."

"Speak for yourself, Violet," said Clarence.

"You can tell Clarence your old secret," said Violet. "Personally, I'm not listening."

Oliver mumbled something.

"Speak up," said Violet. "Clarence can't hear you."

"I don't want to talk about it," said Oliver, and he swam away.

"And we don't want to know about it!" called Violet.

"I wonder what he's up to," said Clarence.

"Me, too," said Violet.

2. A SAFE AND SOUND SECRET

The next day, Oliver was hammering and sawing again. He stopped to rest for a minute, and tossed his hammer on the ground. It made a hollow *klonk*.

"Ouch!" said Clarence.

"Sorry," said Oliver. "Didn't see you."

"As usual," said Clarence.

Oliver started to saw.

"Told anybody your secret yet?" called Clarence.

"Nope," said Oliver.

"That's a shame," Clarence yelled.

Oliver stopped sawing. "Why?" he asked.

"Well," said Clarence, "just supposing a big rock fell on you."

"A big rock?" said Oliver. "Why would that happen?"

"Never mind why," said Clarence. "Just imagine it."

Oliver looked up in the sky. "I can't," he said.

"Well, can you imagine *anything* terrible happening to you?" said Clarence.

Oliver thought for a while. "I could

get lost in the woods and be late for lunch," he said.

"No, no, no," said Clarence. "I mean an accident. Where you get killed."

"Me? Killed?" said Oliver. "I'd hate that."

"The point is," said Clarence, "what would happen to your secret? No one would ever know."

"So what?" said Oliver. "That's the idea of secrets."

"Well, that's all right for boring secrets," said Clarence. "But if it was a really good secret, that would be awful."

"Hmm," said Oliver.

"Which kind is yours?" asked Clarence. "Boring or really good?"

"Well, it's not boring," said Oliver.

"In that case," said Clarence, "I suggest you tell it to somebody you can trust. Somebody who would never ever tell. Then, no matter what happened, your secret would be safe and sound."

"Even if a rock fell on me, eh?" said Oliver, looking up in the sky.

"Right!" said Clarence.

"I'll do it," said Oliver.

"Good!" said Clarence.

"I'll tell Vince," said Oliver.

"Vince!" cried Clarence. "You can't tell Vince. Nobody trusts Vince."

"Who could I tell?" said Oliver.

Clarence looked thoughtful.

"How about you, Clarence?" asked Oliver. "Are you good at keeping secrets?"

"You must be joking," said Clarence. "I'm the *best*." He lowered his voice. "Whisper it, Oliver. . . . You never know who might be listening."

3. THE SECRET
SLIPS OUT

"Hey, Oliver," said Violet later that day. "I hear you're building a ship to sail around the world!" She started to laugh.

"What?" said Oliver, dropping his saw. "Did Clarence tell?"

"It just slipped out," said a voice from the bushes.

"Thanks, Clarence," said Oliver.

"What do you want to sail around the world for, Oliver?" asked Violet, laughing.

"To get away from people like you and Clarence," said Oliver.

"Well!" said Violet. "I hope you leave soon."

"Me, too," said Clarence, coming out of the bushes.

"Have a nice trip, Oliver," said Violet, "and don't hurry back."

"I'm not *coming* back," said Oliver.

"You aren't?" said Clarence.

"No, indeed," said Oliver. "When I get to a place that's beautiful, with lots of rivers and people who are nice, I'm staying there."

"Really?" said Violet. "Well, don't worry about us missing you. I'm sure

another dumb beaver will come along to take your place." Then she marched away.

"Maybe even dumber than you," said Clarence, "though that's hard to believe." Then he marched off, too.

Oliver went back to work.

4. VINCE LENDS A HAND

"Hey, Ludlow!" called Vince. "You're looking good today!"

"Me?" said Ludlow.

"Well, you know—for a fish," said Vince. "What's happening?"

"Tell me something," said Ludlow. "How come you're always diving and swimming around and churning up our pond, Vince?"

"Why not?" asked Vince.

"If I were a frog," said Ludlow, "I'd jump up onto that nice warm land there and get dry in the sun."

"Well, maybe I'll do that," said Vince.

"Good," said Ludlow.

Vince jumped up onto the shore. Violet came by.

"Hey, Violet," said Vince. "Anybody ever tell you you're a really fabulous turkey?"

"Not that I remember," said Violet.

"Well, you are," said Vince, giving her a big smile.

"Please don't smile, Vince," said Violet. "It gives me the willies."

"Sorry," said Vince. "Guess I should lay off the charm. . . ."

"What are you doing up here on the land on a hot day like this?" asked Violet. "If I were you, I'd jump right into that nice cool water. And stay there."

"That's just what I was about to do," said Vince.

He dove into the water, and swam to a lily pad. He climbed up on the leaf. "Nobody minds me sitting *here*, I trust," he said, and shut his eyes. He had started to doze off, when something fluttered past his head. "Huh?" said Vince.

"It's only us, Vince," squeaked Grover, swooping past Vince's nose. "Grover and—"

"—Cheryl," screeched Cheryl, diving in the opposite direction.

"I thought bats liked to sleep in the daytime," said Vince.

"Usually we do," said Cheryl, making a sharp turn, "but sometimes we like to come out and—"

"—catch up on the latest daytime news," said Grover, flying low over Vince's head, and passing Cheryl who was flying in the other direction. Vince turned this way and that, as they crisscrossed back and forth.

"Listen," said Vince, "you're great bats and it's a pleasure talking to you, but it makes me feel like throwing up. Couldn't you just land for a minute?"

"Where?" said Cheryl.

"Here on the lily pad," said Vince, moving over to make room.

"It bobs up and down," said Grover. "Yecchh . . ."

He took off again.

"We're not into landing," said Cheryl.

"Unless we can hang by our toes," said Grover.

"So just give us the highlights of the pond news," said Cheryl, "and we'll head home."

"The big news," said Vince, "is Oliver is building a ship to sail around the world."

"Around the world?" cried Grover. "Oh, wow!"

"Who's going with him?" asked Cheryl.

"I don't know," said Vince.

"I want to go!" said Cheryl.

"Can we get tickets?" said Grover.

"Tickets?" said Vince. "Tickets?"

"Yeah!" said Cheryl. "We want to go around the world, too!"

"Well," said Vince slowly, "tickets are not easy to come by, you understand. You have to know somebody."

"Somebody like you?" said Cheryl.

"Give me a day or two," said Vince. "I'll see what I can do." He gave them a huge smile.

Cheryl and Grover shut their eyes.

When they opened them, Vince was leaping from lily pad to lily pad across the pond, until he disappeared into the tall grass on the far side. The lily pads wobbled on the water.

5. STRANGE SOUNDS

"It certainly is quiet around here," said Violet.

"Oliver must be just about finished with his boat," said Clarence.

"What a relief it will be to have him gone," Violet said.

"Peace at last around the pond," agreed Clarence. "I wonder where he'll settle down."

"I don't care," said Violet, "as long as it's faraway."

"It probably is . . . faraway," said Clarence. "Faraway and romantic and mysterious and beautiful. Not like the pond at all."

Suddenly they heard some strange sounds.

"What in the world is that?" said Violet.

"Could be a very large mosquito," said Clarence.

"Could be somebody sawing a tin can with a rusty saw," said Violet.

"Hold it! Hold it!" said a very small, high voice. The sounds stopped. "Somebody is singing the wrong note! Is it you, Norris?"

"No, sir," said another small voice.

"Morris?" said the first voice.

"Not me," said a new voice.

"It's you, Doris?"

"Nope."

"Boris?"

"No way!"

"Well, let's take it again from the top then," said the first voice. "One, two, and three—" The noise began again.

Violet and Clarence peered around some ferns.

"Oh, for heaven's sake," said Violet, "it's those salamanders!"

"I can't stand that noise! I'm going into my shell," said Clarence, his head disappearing from sight. "Give me a tap on the top when it's over."

Finally the song ended.

"Hi, Violet," said Horace, the leader. "How'd you like it?"

"The end is all right," said Violet.

"We call ourselves 'The Swamp-Tones,'" said Horace. Norris, Morris, Doris, and Boris all smiled and waved. "We can sing at parties and special events," said Horace.

"We could sing at your birthday,

Violet, if you'd like," said Doris. "When is it?"

"Not for a long time," said Violet.

"We could sing for you *now*," said Boris. "What would you like to hear?"

"I have to rush off," said Violet. "But I'm sure Clarence here would like to hear a song."

"But he's in his shell," said Horace.

"Just tap a couple of times on top," called Violet, hurrying away past the ferns. "He'll come out."

"Ready, everybody?" asked Horace. He tapped twice on Clarence's shell. The singing began just as Clarence stuck his head out.

"AaaaaGHHHH!" yelled Clarence, and went back into his shell.

6. READY TO SET SAIL

Oliver's ship was nearly built. He was fixing the mast when Clarence came by.

"I don't mean to interrupt," said Clarence.

"Then don't," said Oliver.

"I was just wondering," said Clarence, "how you know how to go around the world."

"I've got a map," said Oliver.

"Let's see," said Clarence.

Oliver unfolded a big piece of paper.

"What's the circle?" asked Clarence.

"That's the world," said Oliver.

"Oh, I see," said Clarence. "Very round."

"Very," said Oliver.

"What's the little X on the circle?"

"That's us," said Oliver.

"The old pond, eh?"

"Correct," said Oliver. "I plan to sail around the circle. That way I won't get lost."

"Very clever," said Clarence. "What about provisions—food for the trip?"

"I haven't got to that part yet."

"How do you feel about lettuce and tomato sandwiches?" asked Clarence.

"They're okay," said Oliver.

"Good," said Clarence. "I happen to have a bagful behind that tree."

"What for?" asked Oliver.

"Just in case we get hungry going around the world," said Clarence.

"'We'?" said Oliver.

"Well, if you don't want me," said Clarence, "I could take my sandwiches home."

"All ready to set sail," said Oliver

an hour later, "except we don't have a sail."

"A sail is a must, huh?" said Clarence, who was helping. "I don't know how to make one."

"Me, either," said Oliver. "I can't sew."

"I bet Violet could make a sail," said Clarence.

"Darned right I could," said Violet, stepping out of the woods. "How's this?" She unrolled a big sheet, with the words VIOLET II painted on it.

"That's a nice sail," said Oliver. "But what's VIOLET II?"

"The name of the ship," she said. "I'm Violet I. The ship is Violet II."

"The sail looks excellent," said Clarence.

"It better be," said Violet. "I don't sail on any ship that doesn't have a good sail."

"You mean—" Oliver began.

"Hoist the sail and let's get going," said Violet. "I've never been around the world."

7. A NICE FAREWELL

Oliver started to hoist the sail. Then he stopped. "What's that stuff hanging from the yardarm?" he said.

"Looks like some old rags," said Violet.

"Rags!" squeaked Grover. "Don't you know a bat when you see one?"

"Sorry," said Violet.

"We're only trying to keep out of

your way and not be a bother," said Cheryl.

"Did you come to say goodbye?" said Oliver.

"Goodbye?" said Grover. "Certainly not!"

"We're going with you!" said Cheryl.

"Around the world!" said Grover. "Let's go!"

"Wait a minute," said Oliver. "I can't take you two. I'm very sorry, but—"

"You have to take us," screeched Grover. "We have our tickets!"

"Bought and paid for!" cried Cheryl.

"Tickets?" said Oliver.

Suddenly Margaret and Donald and

Kevin and Louise and Edith and Archie and JoAnne and Waylon came running out of the woods.

"I want to ride in front!" shouted Kevin, jumping on board.

"Me, too!" yelled Louise.

"Move over!" cried Archie, pushing Violet to one side.

"Where do you think you're going?" demanded Violet.

"Around the world!" said Waylon, climbing onto the deck.

Margaret landed with a thud on the boat, and knocked Clarence overboard into the water. "Oops," said Margaret, peering over the side. There were bubbles on the water. Then Clarence's head appeared. He was spluttering. "This is outrageous!" he cried.

"Let's get started!" shouted JoAnne, grabbing a rope and pulling. The sail started to go up.

"Let go of that!" cried Oliver.

JoAnne let go, and the sail fell down, ballooning out, covering everybody. There was a big struggle underneath the sail, and lots of muffled shouting. Finally Oliver fought his way out from under and yelled, "Everybody off my ship! Right *now*!"

Kevin rolled out from under the sail. "But we all have tickets, Oliver," he protested.

"You, too?" said Oliver. "Where did you get them?"

Just then there was a loud, high sound. Clarence peered out from beneath the sail. "Oh, no!" he said. "The Swamp-Tones!" He disappeared under the sail again.

The Swamp-Tones were standing on the shore. They began singing a song about ships sailing off into the sunset.

"Quiet!" yelled Oliver.

The Swamp-Tones stopped singing. "Did you say 'Quiet,' Oliver?" asked Horace.

"Yes, I did!" shouted Oliver.

Horace looked hurt. "You didn't like our song?" he said.

"I like it, but I don't want to hear it right now," said Oliver. "I have problems. . . ." He gestured at the lumpy sail heaving and bulging on the deck.

"We thought it would be a nice farewell. . . ." said Horace. "This is the thanks we get," he added, turning to Norris, Boris, Morris, and Doris. They all shrugged.

Oliver managed to pull the sail off the others. "Now what's all this about tickets?" he demanded. "Where did you get them?"

"We bought them from Vince," said Margaret.

"Vince!" said Oliver.

"And they weren't cheap," said Waylon.

"Vince had no business doing that," said Oliver.

"That's Vince for you," said JoAnne.

"That rat," said Edith.

"Please," said Archie, who was a rat.

"I mean skunk," said Edith.

"Hey," said Kevin, who was a skunk. Everybody started arguing and pushing.

"All ashore!" shouted Oliver. "Everybody off the boat—right this minute!"

Grumbling and protesting, the others slowly filed off the ship. Oliver

helped Clarence get aboard. "Stand by to pull up the anchor!" cried Oliver.

"Aye, aye!" said Violet.

"Right, Captain!' said Clarence.

The Swamp-Tones burst into song again, and Oliver hoisted the sail. "Now!" he cried. Clarence and Violet hauled in the anchor, and the *Violet II* was underway, moving out from the shore.

8. DOWN THE RIVER

A light wind came up and filled the sail. The ship glided briskly across the pond. "This is wonderful!" cried Oliver, steering. "Smell the salt air!"

"Salt air is on oceans," said Violet, sitting on the bow.

"We must be getting near one," said Clarence. "Who's for a sandwich?"

"Me," said Oliver. "Travel really gives you an appetite."

They ate the sandwiches as Oliver steered the ship out of the pond and down a broad river.

"There's a whale!" cried Clarence.

"That's a rock," said Violet.

"Very similar," said Clarence. He looked at the woods going by. "Wow," he said, "I like the world better than the pond. More to see."

"Gorgeous," said Violet.

"Look at the sky," said a squeaky voice.

"And above that, the water," added another. "What a view."

"The water *above* the sky?" said Oliver.

He looked up. Cheryl and Grover were hanging upside down from the yardarm again. "Oh, no," said Oliver.

"What's the matter, Oliver?" asked Cheryl. "You want us to leave?"

"I guess you can stay," said Oliver. "If you keep out of the way and be quiet."

"Are *we* the ones who shout and yell?" said Grover.

"Are *we* the ones who get in the way and make trouble?" said Cheryl.

"Really," said Grover.

"Really," said Cheryl.

It was very quiet for a while, with only the sound of the water glopping against the hull.

"Where do you think we are now?" asked Violet presently.

Oliver looked at the map, then out at the trees. "I'm not positive," he said, "but this could be Australia."

"Wow," said Clarence.

9. A STOWAWAY

"Something's strange," said Oliver, looking at the sail.

"Like what?" asked Clarence.

"Well, the wind is getting stronger, but the boat is moving slower," said Oliver.

"That *is* strange," said Clarence.

"And the rudder doesn't move the way it should," said Oliver.

66

Violet looked down over the stern. "Are there supposed to be green fingers attached to the rudder?" she asked.

"Green fingers?" said Oliver. "Nope."

"Well, there are," said Violet. "Long green fingers."

Oliver looked down. "Oh-oh," he said. "Vince . . ."

Vince's head came up out of the water. "Well, well," said Vince. "Look who's here—my old friends Oliver and Violet and—"

"Vince!" said Clarence. "Not *Vince*!"

"Let go of the rudder, Vince, and go back to the pond where you belong!" said Oliver.

"I can't do that," said Vince. "I'm not popular there."

"You're not popular here, either," said Violet.

"I know, I know," said Vince, suddenly starting to blubber. "I'm not popular anywhere. . . ."

"Stop that," said Clarence.

"All I want is to have a few friends and maybe go around the world," moaned Vince. "Is that too much to ask?"

"Yes!" yelled Clarence.

"Go away, Vince," said Violet.

"I can't," said Vince. "It's too far to swim." He smiled. "Just let me hang on here. I won't bother you."

"Ooh, that *smile*," groaned Violet, looking away.

"I don't know what to do," said Oliver. "Maybe we should take a vote on whether or not to let him stay."

"No! No!" shouted Vince. "Don't vote!"

Just then, Cheryl called down from the yardarm. "There's something up ahead," she said. "I hear it."

"I hear something, too," said Violet. They all listened.

"It sounds like the mighty Pacific crashing on a distant shore," said Clarence.

"It sounds more like a waterfall to me," said Oliver. "If it is, we're in trouble."

"We'll go take a look," said Cheryl, flapping away.

"And we'll report back what we see," said Grover, following Cheryl.

"We're moving faster," said Violet.

"A lot faster," said Oliver.

10. TROUBLE AHEAD

"Maybe you should hit the brakes, Oliver," said Clarence.

"Ships don't have brakes," said Oliver.

"Can't you take down the sail?" asked Violet.

"Yup," said Oliver. "I can." He pulled down the sail. The boat slowed a little bit.

"If there's anything I can't stand," said Violet to Clarence, "it's going around the world on a ship with a dumb captain."

Just then Cheryl and Grover came flying back.

"It's a big waterfall, all right!" squealed Grover.

"And you're headed directly toward it!" squeaked Cheryl.

They all stared ahead toward where

the river narrowed between tall trees and disappeared. They could see the water rushing over the edge.

"We're going to go over that waterfall," said Violet. "No two ways about that."

"Maybe we should abandon ship," said Clarence.

"I can't swim," said Violet.

"I can," said Clarence, "but this current is too fast for me."

"Who's going to save us?" said Violet. "Oliver?"

"Please," said Oliver. "I'm thinking."

"Well, think faster!" cried Violet.

"This is as fast as I think," said Oliver. "Don't rush me."

"*I*'ll save you!" said a loud voice from the stern.

"Who said that?" asked Clarence.

"I—I think *I* did," said Vince.

"You?" said Oliver. "What can you do?"

"I can swim around to the front of the boat, and hang on and kick as hard as I can," said Vince. "Maybe that will push the boat away from the f-falls."

"It won't work, Vince," said Oliver.

"Oh, I realize it's extremely dangerous," said Vince, "but don't try to s-stop me."

"I'm not trying to stop you," said Oliver.

"You aren't?" said Vince. "Don't *you* try to stop me, either, Clarence," he added.

"I'm not," said Clarence.

"And don't you try, Violet," said Vince.

"Who, me?" said Violet.

There was a pause.

"How about those bats up there?" asked Vince. "Do they want to try and stop me?"

"No," said Cheryl.

"Go right ahead," said Grover.

"I see," said Vince. "Well, here goes!" He let go of the rudder and swam around to the bow of the boat, half-carried by the current. He reached

up to grab the side, but the fast-moving
water pulled him away.

"Vince!" cried Violet. "Come
back!"

Vince made a gulping noise that
sounded like "Help!" His eyes got
bigger and bigger. Then he was swept

away down the river toward the waterfall.

"He's going over!" shouted Clarence.

For an instant, Vince's feet could be
seen kicking in the air. Then they were
gone.

Violet, Clarence, and Oliver stared at the place where Vince had been. "He tried to save *us*," said Clarence.

"I can't believe it," said Violet.

"I hate to say so," said Clarence, "but Vince was a rare frog."

"I'm afraid you're right," said Violet. She looked down the river. "But what I want to know is—who's going to save us now?"

11. TURTLES DON'T SNIFFLE

Oliver was standing on the bow, frowning. Suddenly he dived overboard and swam away.

"Oliver!" shouted Clarence. "Don't leave us!"

"Isn't that the limit?" said Violet. "The captain leaving the passengers?

We never should have trusted that dumb beaver."

"I think we'll be heading home now," called Cheryl from the yardarm. "Bye, all!"

"We wish you lots of luck," said Grover. They both flew away.

"*I*'d like to go back to the pond, too," said Clarence in a quavery voice.

"Too late now," said Violet. "I'm going to crawl under the sail and shut my eyes."

"Move over," said Clarence. "I'm going to join you."

Even under the sail they could hear the waterfall getting louder and louder. The boat moved faster.

"Do I hear crying, Clarence?" asked Violet.

"None of your business," said Clarence. He sniffled. "I wasn't planning on this," he said. "Turtles are supposed to live for years and years and years."

"There are exceptions to every rule," said Violet. "Stop sniffling."

Suddenly they heard a grinding noise, a splitting sound, and a big splash. The ship bumped to a stop. Violet lifted the sail and peered out. "Well!" she said.

Clarence looked out, too. The ship was resting against a tree trunk that was lying across the top of the water-fall. "Saved!" cried Clarence.

"All ashore!" cried Oliver. He was standing on the stump of the tree on the shore. There were chips of wood all around him.

"You chewed down that tree, Oliver?" said Violet. "That was fast chewing."

"I know," said Clarence. "My teeth are killing me."

Clarence and Violet stepped from

the ship onto the tree trunk, and walked ashore. "That was smart, Oliver," said Violet.

"Did you say 'smart'?" said Oliver.

"Yes, I did," said Violet. "But next time you go around the world, you need a better map."

"One that shows waterfalls," said Clarence.

"Wow!" said a voice. "What a ride!"

They all turned around and saw Vince, soaking wet, crawling up onto the bank. "Is that you, Vince?" cried Violet.

"Are you all right?" asked Clarence.

Vince nodded. "I'd like to go over those falls again. What a thrill!"

"Thanks for trying to save us, Vince," said Oliver. "That was very brave."

"I know," said Vince. "I *know*." He gave a very big smile.

"Oh, my," said Violet.

"Guess we better head back to the pond," said Oliver.

"What about your ship?" asked Clarence.

"I'll just leave it where it is," said Oliver. "It's a pretty good start for a dam."

12. WELCOME HOME

"Shhh, here they come," whispered Grover. He was hanging upside down from a branch high over the pond.

"One, two, three—" said Cheryl. *"Now!"*

"WELCOME HOME!" shouted all the animals, who were gathered at the edge of the pond.

"How did you know we were coming back so soon?" asked Violet.

"Cheryl and Grover," said Margaret. "They flew in and told us."

"We watched you get safely off the ship," said Cheryl.

"Then we came back to arrange a welcome," added Grover.

"Very nice," said Clarence. Oliver nodded.

"There's a big picnic supper for everybody over by the willow trees," said Margaret.

"Me included?" asked Vince.

"Forgive and forget," said Donald.

"Really?" said Vince.

"We're not very mad at you anymore," said JoAnne.

"Well, in that case," said Vince, "I'd like to do something nice for all of you."

"Such as?" said Edith.

"I'd be willing to make a speech after supper," said Vince, "if everybody insists."

"Speech?" said Edith. "About what?"

"About my incredible and amazing trip down the river," said Vince, "and about how I was the brave hero."

"No, thanks!" cried Margaret.

"Not on your life!" said Edith.

Suddenly there was a strange, high sound. "What's that?" asked Clarence.

"That's our special treat for you and Oliver and Violet," said Margaret.

"Oh, wow," said Clarence. "What is it?"

"The Swamp-Tones!" cried Margaret. "They've agreed to sing a lot of songs!"

Clarence groaned, and started to go into his shell. "Stop that," said Violet, "and cheer up." Clarence came out again. "You know," said Violet, turning to Oliver, "it wouldn't be too hard to make a new sail."

"It wouldn't be too hard to make some more sandwiches, either," said Clarence.

"Well, I've still got my hammer and nails," said Oliver. "And there's plenty of wood."

"Maybe we could start at the far side of the waterfall," said Violet.

Vince's eyes got wide. "You're going to try again?" he said. "What a great idea!"

"The *Violet III*," said Violet. "I like the sound of that."

"Maybe *I* could be captain this time," said Vince. "We could call it the *Vince I*."

"No!" cried Clarence.

"I prefer *Violet III*," said Violet.

"Me, too," said Oliver.

"Just an idea," said Vince, with a big smile.

Violet winced.

"Supper's ready, everybody!" yelled Grover, zooming out of the willow tree.

"So come and get it!" cried Cheryl, and all the animals rushed toward the picnic.